Library of Congress Cataloging in Publication Data
Roberts, Bethany. Camel caravan / by Bethany Roberts and Patricia Hubbell;
pictures by Cheryl Munro Taylor. – 1st ed. p. cm.
Summary: Tired of carrying their burdens in the desert, the camels sneak away
from the caravan and have exciting adventures as they explore other ways to travel.
[1. Camels—Fiction. 2. Vehicles—Fiction. 3. Deserts—Fiction. 4. Stories in rhyme.] I. Hubbell, Patricia.
II. Taylor, Cheryl Munro, 1957– ill. III. Title
PZ8.3.R5295Cam 1996 [E]—dc20 95-38257 CIP AC
ISBN 0-688-13939-6 (tr.) — ISBN 0-688-13940-X (lib. bdg.)

10 9 8 7 6 5 4 3 2 1
First edition

For Megan —B.R. and P.H.

For Ken and Ruthann with love —C.M.T.

Bethany Roberts & Patricia Hubbell

CAMEL CARAVAN

Pictures by **Cheryl Munro Taylor**

TAMBOURINE BOOKS  NEW YORK

The camel caravan
Crosses the desert,
CLUMP,
CLUMP,
CLUMP!

Hot! Dry!
Dusty! Slow!
GRUMP,
GRUMP,
GRUMP!

To greener pastures
Off they go,
THUMP,
THUMP,
THUMP!

Catch a boxcar,
Spooky! Dark!
BUMP,
BUMP,
BUMP!

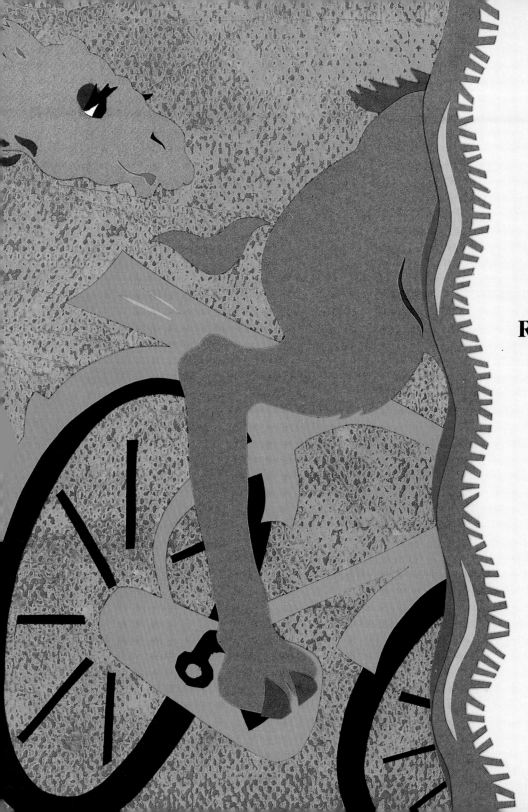

Ride their bikes,
Pedal fast,
PUMP,
PUMP,
PUMP!

Snooze and snore,
Bees sting,
LUMP,
LUMP,
LUMP!

Go by bus,
Passengers fuss,
WHUMP,
WHUMP,
WHUMP!

Sail a boat,
Waves are rough,
RUMP,
RUMP,
RUMP!

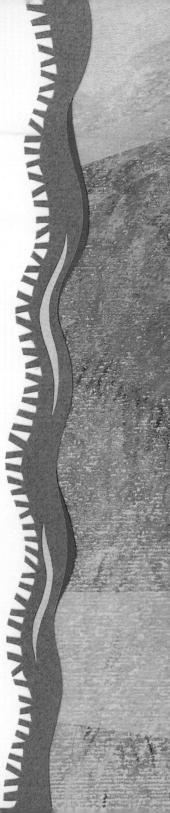

Travel by truck,
Noisy! Crowded!
SLUMP,
SLUMP,
SLUMP!

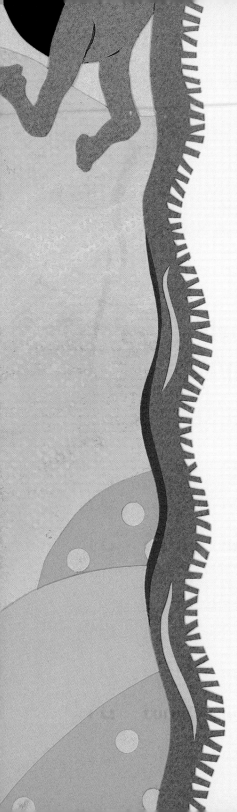

Engine trouble!
Parachute out!
JUMP,
JUMP,
JUMP!

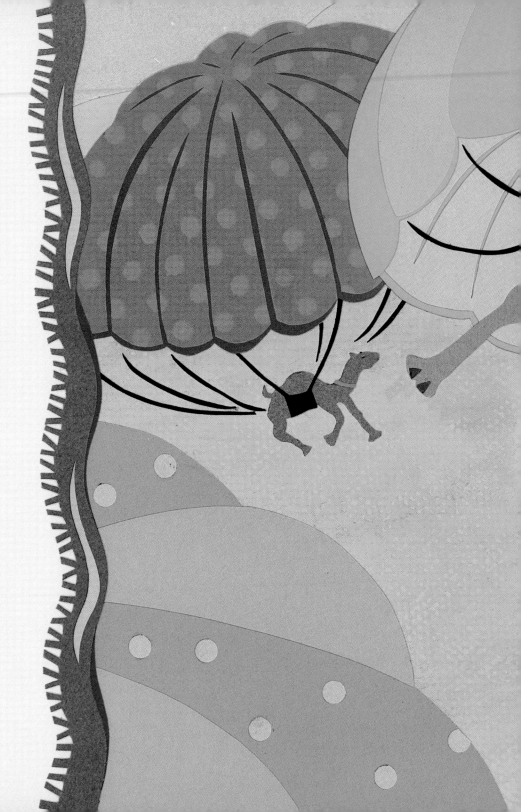

Cranky camels
Jam on a plane,
STUMP,
STUMP,
STUMP!

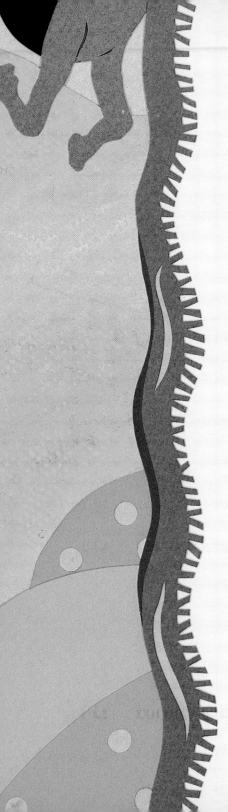

Engine trouble!
Parachute out!
JUMP,
JUMP,
JUMP!

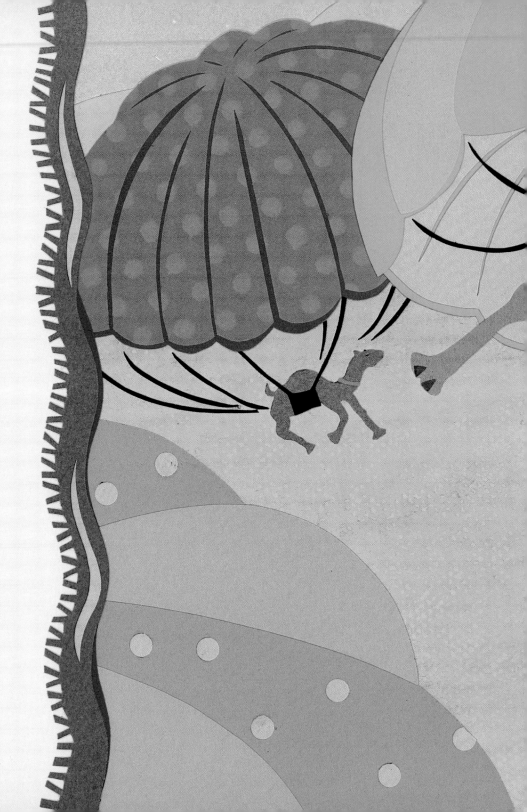